KIJO
the Baby Gorilla

by
Jill Jago & Gerry Livingston

MACDONALD YOUNG BOOKS

Kijo the baby gorilla lives in the big dark African forest. When his mother goes looking for berries and fruit to eat, Kijo always goes with her. He clings tight to the thick fur on her back.

Kijo loves playing hide-and-seek with his brother and sister, round and round among the tall trees and thick ferns.
Life in the forest is fun!

While the young gorillas play,
the father gorilla keeps watch.
Suddenly he smells danger.

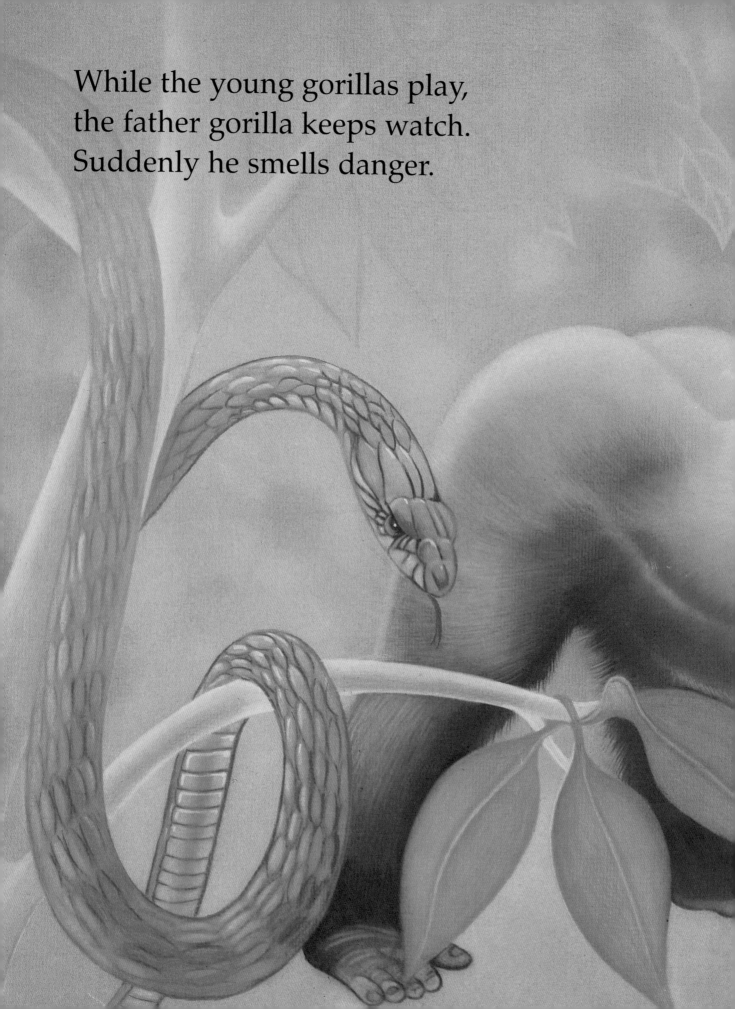

Men!
They are coming closer and closer,
hunting for gorillas.
Father gorilla beats his chest and roars.

WRAAGGHH!

Quick, quick Kijo!
Father gorilla races away with the little ones,
into the thickest part of the forest,
where the men cannot find them.

At last Kijo's father decides it is safe to stop.
But Kijo cannot see his mother anywhere.
Where is she? What will he do without
the warm comfort of her fur?

Kijo creeps off to look for his lost mother.

Who's this?

It's only a pangolin, Kijo!
A pangolin won't harm a baby gorilla.

Rustle, rustle.

The noise in the bushes makes Kijo jump.
But it's just a tiny antelope. She prances
towards him and runs away again.
She is far more frightened than Kijo.

Kijo hears another noise in the grass.
Something is creeping closer and closer . . .

It's a leopard! She's looking for something tasty to give her hungry cubs for supper.

Run, Kijo! Run!

Kijo is too scared to move.
The leopard is ready to spring.
Suddenly she pricks up her ears.
Her cubs are calling her.
With a snarl, she turns and bounds away.

Poor little Kijo is shaking with fright.
He is lost and very hungry, and he
needs his mother to protect him.
But Kijo is so tired. He just curls up
in a sad little ball and goes to sleep.

He sleeps for a long time until …

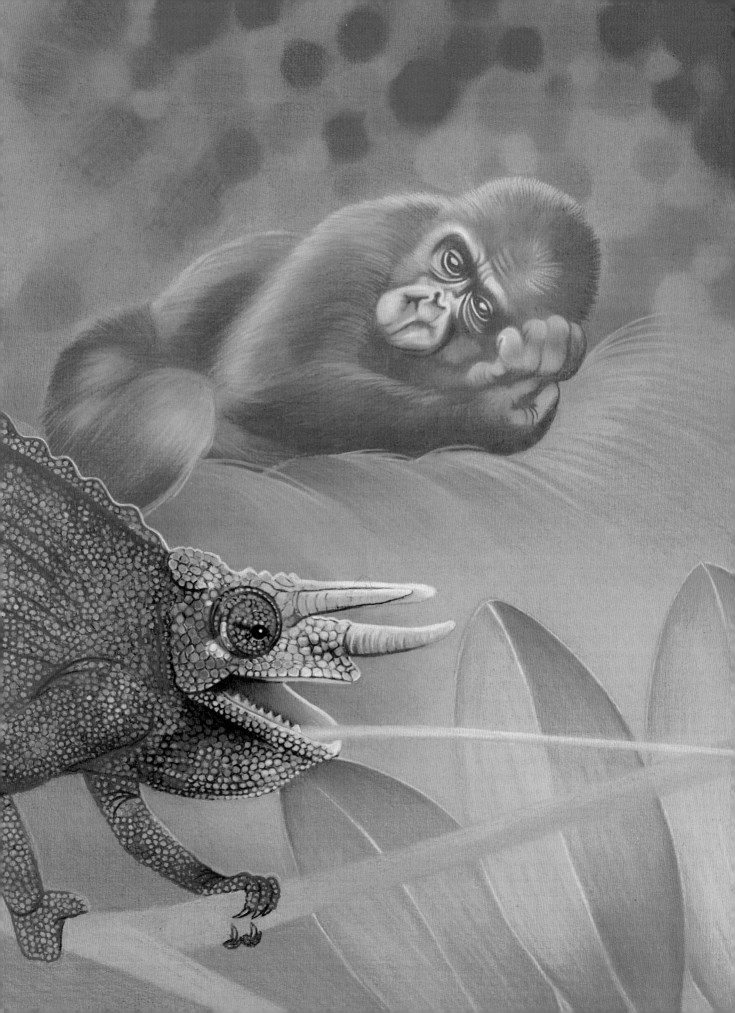

... someone wakes him.

It's a big gorilla - is she his mother?
No, she smells different. She knows
Kijo isn't her baby, and she walks away.

Kijo begins to whimper . . .

. . . and the big gorilla comes back.
Very gently, she picks Kijo up and
cradles him in her arms.
She has found a new baby.
And Kijo has found a new mother.